LOVABYE DRAGON

Barbara Joosse

illustrated by Randy Cecil

CANDLEWICK PRESS

Once there was a girl
an all-alone girl
in her own little bed
in her own little room
in her own little castle
who didn't have
a dragon
for a friend.

And there was a dragon

   an all-alone dragon

in his big dragon nest

in his big dragon cave

in his big dragon mountain

who dreamed

   of a girl

      for a friend.

Oh, she cried silver tears

    many, many tears

so wishing for a dragon

so *lonely* for a dragon

and they trickled down the stairs

past a teeny-tiny mouse in his teeny-tiny house

past a boat in the moat

past a frog in the bog

round a bend in the glen

to the mountain with the cave

and the dragon.

Snore-asleep was the dragon

dream-asleep was the dragon

but the trickle of tears

   little *tickle* of tears

woke him up.

Gluk!

Dragon followed the trail

the little silver trail

round the bend in the glen

past the frog in the bog

past the boat in the moat

past the teeny-tiny mouse

in his teeny-tiny house . . .

to the castle and the room and the girl.

Came a rumble and tumble
that might be a giant but it wasn't
and might be a monster but it wasn't
and might be a dragon . . .

AND IT WAS!

"I am here!" roared Dragon.

"You're a dear!" whispered Girl.

"I found you!" roared Dragon.

"As I wished," whispered Girl.

Now they've found each other
and found *out* about each other
so they marched and they sang
all the live-long day

and they slid and they hid

till the deep, dark night.

All right.

On the outside, Girl is little.

On the outside, Dragon's biggle.

But they're *just* the same size

   exactly the same size

in the middle.

Dragon makes a fire

such a roasty, toasty fire

and he roars a dragon roar

such a rum-below *roar*

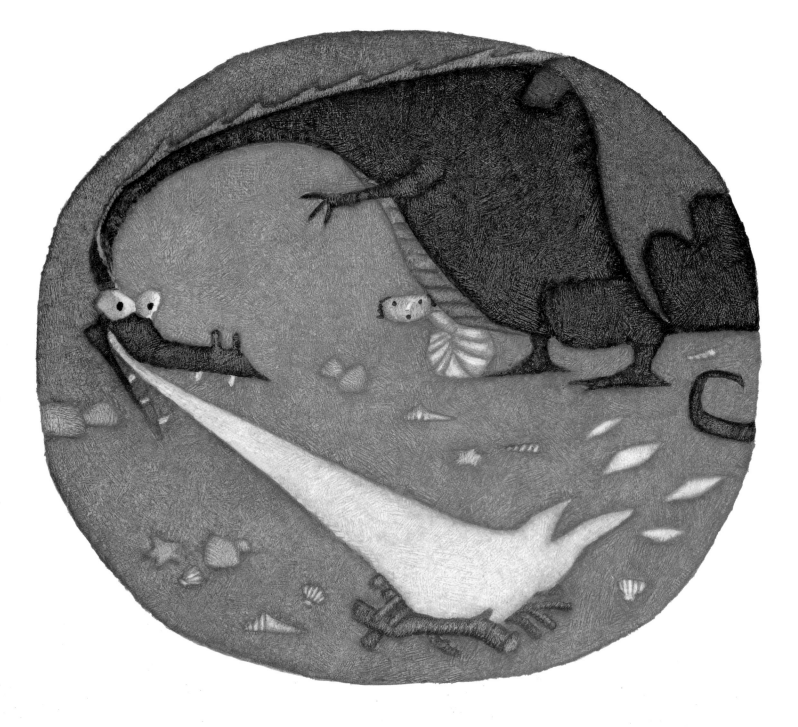

that the giants and the monsters nevermore, nevermore
and she's lonely for a dragon nevermore.

Now she sings little songs

little lovabye songs

and he wraps his tail around her

so gently, all around her.

Now they're friends.

Best friends.

Forever friends.

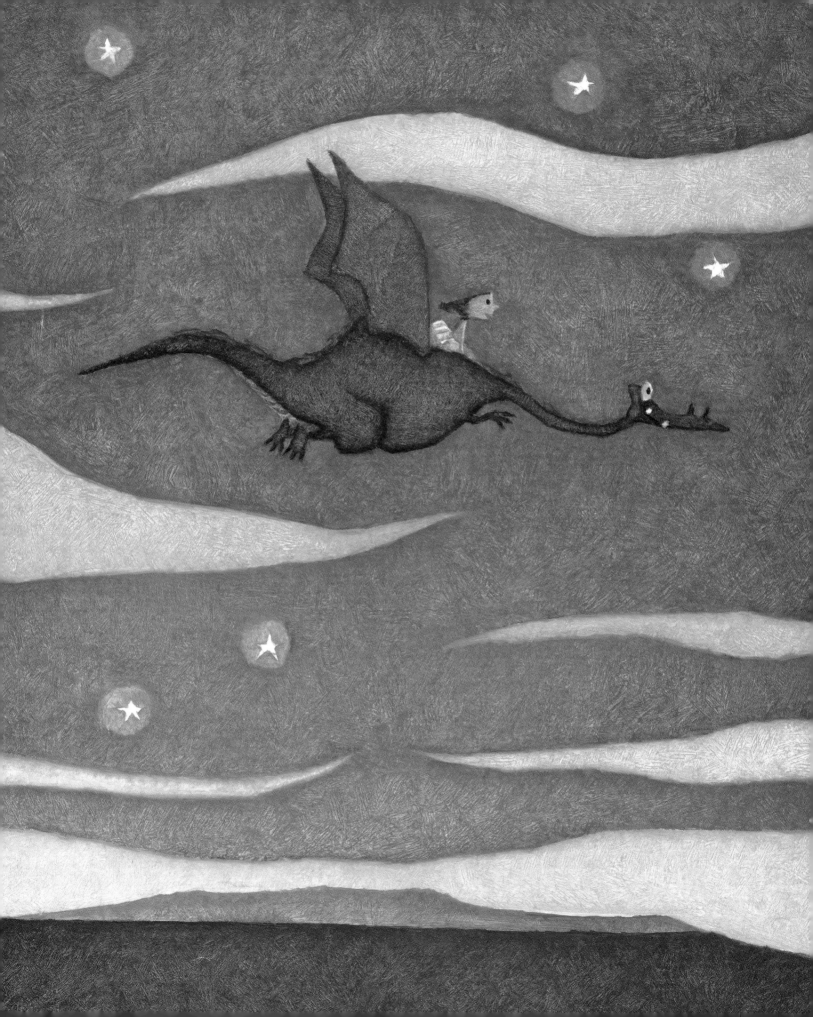

For Marina and Lucia,
and all the Dragons and all the Girls
B. J.

For Lucy
R. C.

Text copyright © 2012 by Barbara Joosse
Illustrations copyright © 2012 by Randy Cecil

First edition 2012

Library of Congress Cataloging-in-Publication Data is available.

Library of Congress Catalog Card Number pending

ISBN 978-0-7636-5408-5

12 13 14 15 16 17 CCP 10 9 8 7 6 5 4 3 2 1

Printed in Shenzhen, Guangdong, China

This book was typeset in Horley Old Style Semibold.
The illustrations were done in oil.

Candlewick Press
99 Dover Street
Somerville, Massachusetts 02144

visit us at www.candlewick.com